ABOUT THE BANK STREET READY-TO-READ SERIES

Seventy years of educational research and innovative teaching have given the Bank Street College of Education the reputation as America's most trusted name in early childhood education.

Because no two children are exactly alike in their development, we have designed the *Bank Street Ready-to-Read* series in three levels to accommodate the individual stages of reading readiness of children ages four through eight.

- ○ *Level 1:* GETTING READY TO READ—read-alouds for children who are taking their first steps toward reading.
- ○ *Level 2:* READING TOGETHER—for children who are just beginning to read by themselves but may need a little help.
- ○ *Level 3:* I CAN READ IT MYSELF—for children who can read independently.

Our three levels make it easy to select the books most appropriate for a child's development and enable him or her to grow with the series step by step. The *Bank Street Ready-to-Read* books also overlap and reinforce each other, further encouraging the reading process.

We feel that making reading fun and enjoyable is the single most important thing that you can do to help children become good readers. And we hope you'll be a part of Bank Street's long tradition of learning through sharing.

The Bank Street College of Education

To Fred, who shared the experience
—B.B.

To the Dickermans
—E.A.M.

BEAVERS BEWARE!

A Bantam Little Rooster Book / February 1992

Little Rooster is a trademark of Bantam Books,
a division of Bantam Doubleday Dell Publishing Group, Inc.

Series graphic design by Alex Jay / Studio J

Special thanks to James A. Levine, Betsy Gould,
and Sally Doherty.

Library of Congress Cataloging-in-Publication Data

Brenner, Barbara
Beavers beware! / by Barbara Brenner;
illustrated by Emily Arnold McCully.
p. cm. — (Bank Street Ready-to-Read)
"A Byron Preiss book,"
"A Bantam Little Rooster Book."
Summary: A family with a house on the river finds
two beavers cutting down trees and building
a lodge on their dock.
ISBN 0-553-07498-9. — ISBN 0-553-35386-1 (pbk.)
1. Beavers—Juvenile fiction. [1. Beavers — Fiction.]
I. McCully, Emily Arnold, ill.   II. Title.   III. Series.
PZ10.3.B753Be   1992
[E]—dc20
91-10598   CIP   AC

Published simultaneously in the United States and Canada

Bantam Books are published by Bantam Books, a division of Bantam Doubleday
Dell Publishing Group, Inc. Its trademark, consisting of the words "Bantam
Books" and the portrayal of a rooster, is Registered in U.S. Patent and Trademark
Office and in other countries. Marca Registrada. Bantam Books, 666 Fifth Avenue,
New York, New York 10103.

Bank Street Ready-to-Read™

BEAVERS BEWARE!

by Barbara Brenner
Illustrated by Emily Arnold McCully

A Byron Preiss Book

A BANTAM LITTLE ROOSTER BOOK
NEW YORK · TORONTO · LONDON · SYDNEY · AUCKLAND

This is our house
by the river.
This is our dock,
where the story begins.

One day we find
two little sticks lying
on the dock.
We know right away
they are not any old sticks.
They are too clean and slick.

The next day three more sticks
show up.
They're clean and slick, too.

I say, "What happened to the bark
on these sticks?"
Dad says,
"Maybe an animal ate it."
We throw the sticks away.

The next day there are
more sticks on the dock,
and a big branch, too.
We take the sticks away.
We drag the branch away.

Pretty soon there are
ten sticks, two branches,
and a big tree on the dock.
They are each cut to a point.

"What animal could do this?"
I ask.
"An animal with sharp teeth,"
my dad says.

Every day we take away
sticks, branches, and trees.
But the next day new ones
always show up.

"I'd like to see that animal," I say.
Mom says, "It must come
at night."

Then one day I am
swimming off the dock.
WHOOSH!
Two heads pop up
out of the water.
I get a quick look at
brown fur and round heads.
I see a flash of orange teeth.
SMACK!
A tail slaps the water.
They dive and are gone.
I know what they are.
BEAVERS!

I tell Mom and Dad.
"There are two beavers
at the dock!"
"Beavers eat bark," Dad says.
Mom says, "And they build
with sticks and branches.
They must be building a lodge."

By the next week the lodge
is taller than my dad.
Mom says,
"If you put beavers by water,
they'll start building.
And once they get going,
they won't stop."

The week after that
the beavers stuff the cracks
in the lodge with clam shells
and old rags and string.
It begins to look like a junk pile.

The week after that
they begin to build under the dock.
Mom dives down to take a look.

"There's a tunnel down here,"
she calls.
"It leads up to that space
under the dock.
It's dry there.
That must be where they sleep."
"Pretty clever," I say.
"Pretty messy," says Dad.

The next week the beavers
put mud all over their lodge.
They put their own smell
on the mud
to keep other beavers away.
Dad says, "That smell would keep
anybody away."

20

Now the beavers begin
to cut down big trees.
Mom gets mad about the trees.
"Animals have rights," I say.
"Trees have rights, too," she says.

The beavers move in.
By day they sleep under our dock.
At dusk they eat the water plants.
At night they cut down our trees.

"This is war," my dad says.
"I'm calling the game warden.
He can trap the beavers alive
and move them."

"What about animal rights?" I ask.
"What about people rights?"
Mom asks.

But that night
there is a storm.
The wind howls.

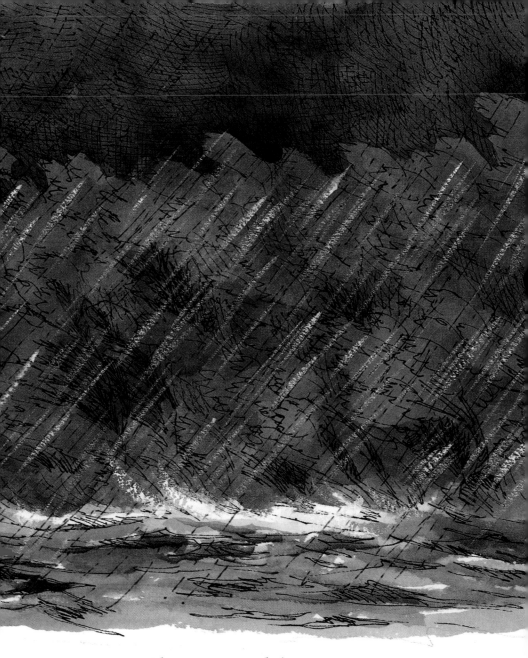

There are big waves
on the river.
Sometime that night
the dock floats loose.

In the morning
everything is gone—
dock, sticks, mud,
trees, junk, smell—
and the beavers!
I say to Dad,
"If this is war,
the beavers win!"

I still think about those beavers.
I think of them
floating down the river
on our dock.
Or maybe they're chewing away
with those big orange teeth,
building a new lodge.

We're building, too.
We're building a new dock.
Only this time —
no beavers allowed.